NICKELODEON
WONDER
PETS!™

Floppy's First Sleepover

adapted by Dustin Ferrer
Based on the screenplay "Help the Houseguest" written by Billy Aronson
illustrated by Michael Zodorozny, Little Airplane Productions

SIMON SPOTLIGHT/NICKELODEON
New York   London   Toronto   Sydney

Based on the TV series *Wonder Pets!*™ as seen on Nickelodeon®

Simon Spotlight/Nickelodeon
An imprint of Simon & Schuster Children's Publishing Division
1230 Avenue of the Americas, New York, New York 10020
© 2010 Viacom International Inc. All rights reserved. NICKELODEON, Nick Jr., *Wonder Pets!*, and all related titles, logos, and characters
are trademarks of Viacom International Inc. All rights reserved, including the right of reproduction in whole or in part in any form.
SIMON SPOTLIGHT and colophon are registered trademarks of Simon & Schuster, Inc.
Manufactured in the United States of America / 0810 LAK
10 9 8 7 6 5 4 3 2
ISBN 978-1-4169-9756-6

Linny the Guinea Pig, Turtle Tuck and Ming-Ming Duckling were sitting quietly in their cages. Suddenly, the red tin-can phone started to ring!

Ring-ring!

Ring-ring!

The Wonder Pets rushed to answer the phone. They sang,
"*The phone! The phone is ringing!*
The phone! We'll be right there!
The phone! The phone is ringing!
There's an animal in trouble somewhere!"

Ring-ring!

Ring-ring!

Linny picked up the tin-can phone.
"Tuck," she said. "This call is for you!"
"It's Floppy the Circus Elephant!" said Ming-Ming.
"Wahoo!" yelled Tuck.
"I just knew Floppy
would call!"

Tuck looked inside the phone and saw his friend.
"Hi, Floppy! Are you in town?" he asked.
"Yes!" said Floppy. "And my mom says I can sleep
over at your school!"
"Great! Come on over!" said Tuck.

Tuck was very excited about his first sleepover!
He sang,
"Floppy's sleeping over!
Oh, yeah! That's right!
Floppy's sleeping over!
Right here! Tonight!"

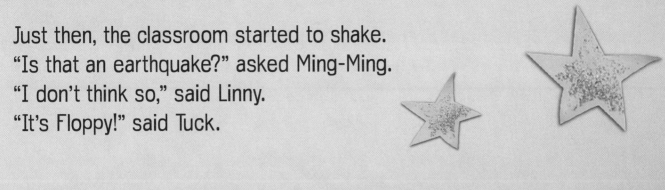

Just then, the classroom started to shake.
"Is that an earthquake?" asked Ming-Ming.
"I don't think so," said Linny.
"It's Floppy!" said Tuck.

Floppy had never been to the classroom before.
Tuck couldn't wait to show him around!
"This is where we make the Flyboat!" said Tuck.
"Look Tuckster," said Floppy. "I made
a pie boat!"

Next, Tuck showed Floppy the fabric scrap box.
"This is where we try on all kinds of clothes!" said Tuck.
"Look!" said Floppy. "I've got clothes on my nose!"
Tuck and Floppy laughed until their tummies hurt.

After looking around the classroom, Floppy was in the mood for a snack. "Do you have any peanuts?" he asked.

"I'm sorry," said Tuck. "We don't have peanuts in the classroom." Floppy felt sad. "Oh. We always have peanuts at the circus. I miss the circus!" said Floppy.

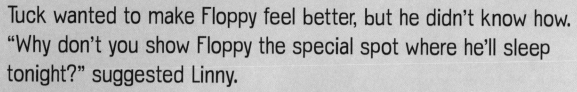

Tuck wanted to make Floppy feel better, but he didn't know how.
"Why don't you show Floppy the special spot where he'll sleep
tonight?" suggested Linny.
"Good idea!" said Tuck. "I'll show him the puffy blankets!"
"I love puffy blankets!" said Floppy.
Tuck brought Floppy over to the pile of
puffy blankets.

"Here's the special spot where you'll sleep tonight," said Tuck.
But Floppy was still sad.
"At the circus, I always sleep under a big tent!" he said. "I really miss the circus!"

Tuck still didn't know how to cheer up Floppy.
"Maybe Floppy will feel better if we sing
him a lullaby!" said Ming-Ming.
"Good idea!" said Linny.

The Wonder Pets sang,
"Rockaby, elephant! Rockaby!
Rest each ear and shut each eye!
All day long you're spry and spunky.
But now it's time to rest your head.
Lay down your trunky!"

Oh, no! Floppy started crying!
"That's the same lullaby my mom
sings to me at the circus," he said.
"I really, really miss the circus."
Floppy wanted to go home.
"This is serious!" said Ming-Ming.

"I know!" said Tuck. "What if we make the classroom more like Floppy's home?"
"Yeah!" said Ming-Ming. "We can change the classroom to be more like the circus."
"Let's do it, Wonder Pets!" said Linny.

First, Ming-Ming used a sheet to make Floppy a tent.
"Step right this way!" said Ming-Ming.
The tent made Floppy feel at home!

"This is just like the tent I sleep
in at the circus!" he said.

Next, Tuck gave Floppy a special snack.
"Here, Floppy!" said Tuck. "It's popcorn and celery!"
"Ooh!" said Floppy. "They have popcorn at the circus, too!"
Ming-Ming whispered, "I think Floppy's starting to feel better!"

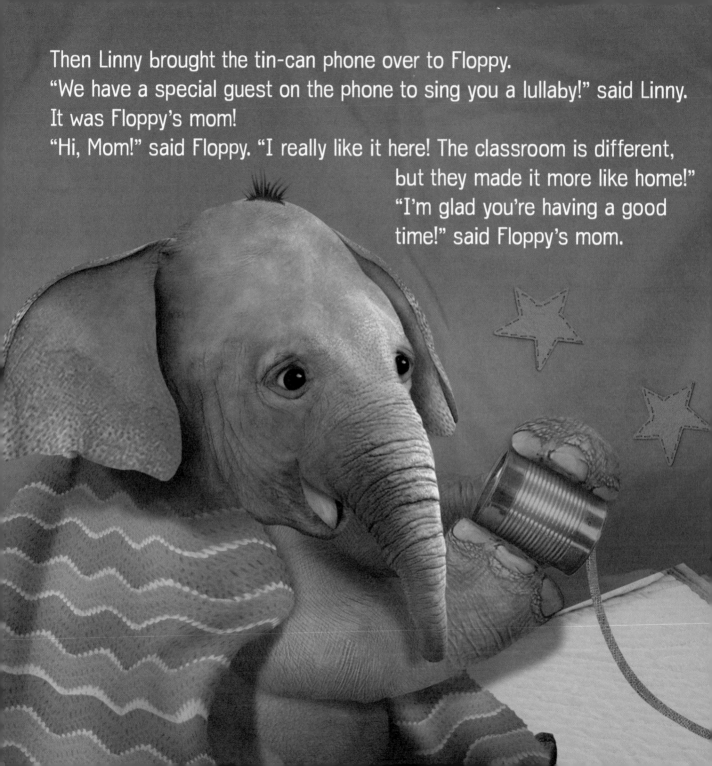

Then Linny brought the tin-can phone over to Floppy.
"We have a special guest on the phone to sing you a lullaby!" said Linny.
It was Floppy's mom!
"Hi, Mom!" said Floppy. "I really like it here! The classroom is different, but they made it more like home!"
"I'm glad you're having a good time!" said Floppy's mom.

It was time for Floppy's lullaby.
Floppy's mom sang,
"Rockabye, elephant! Rockabye!
Rest each ear and shut each eye!
All day long you're spry and spunky.
But now it's time to rest your head.
Lay down your trunky!"

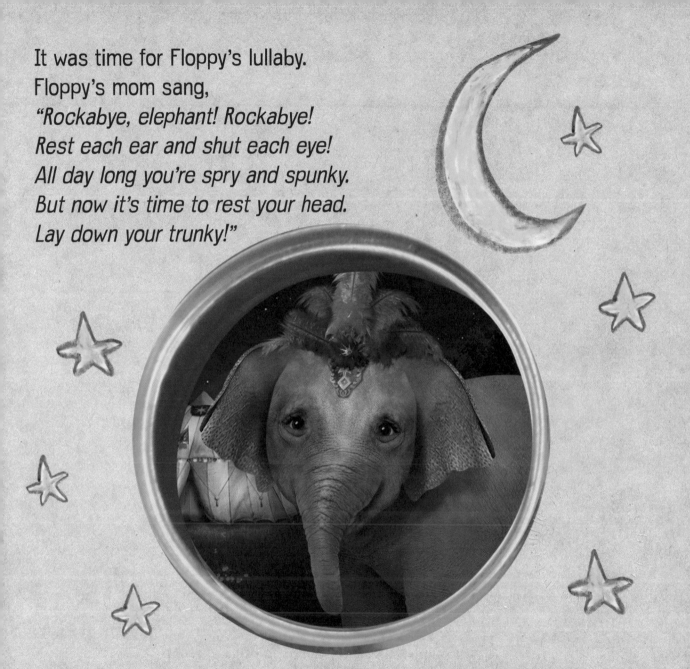

"This lullaby is making me sleepy," said Floppy, "just like it does at the circus."

Floppy wasn't homesick anymore, and he fell fast asleep!
"It was a great sleepover after all," said Tuck.
"It sure was!" said Ming-Ming.
The Wonder Pets were feeling tired too. They pulled up the covers and shut their eyes.
Linny whispered, "Sweet dreams, Wonder Pets."

LITTLE CRITTER'S
ADVENTURE STORYBOOK